This book belongs to:

_____

A catalogue record for this book is available from the British Library

Published by Ladybird Books Ltd
80 Strand, London, WC2R 0RL
A Penguin Company

2 4 6 8 10 9 7 5 3 1
© LADYBIRD BOOKS LTD MMVIII
LADYBIRD and the device of a Ladybird are trademarks of Ladybird Books Ltd

ISBN: 978-1-40930-009-0

Printed in China

my favourite

# RHYMES
# TO SHARE

Illustrated by

Miriam Latimer, Virginia Allyn,
Siobhan Harrison, Kanako Usui, Fernando Luiz,
Natascia Ugliano, Ook Hallbjorn, Andrew Rowland,
Kirsteen Harris-Jones and Holly Surplice

Teddy bear, teddy bear, turn around,

Teddy bear, teddy bear, touch the ground.

Teddy bear, teddy bear, climb the stairs,

Teddy bear, teddy bear, say your prayers.

Teddy bear, teddy bear, turn out the light,

Teddy bear, teddy bear, say goodnight.

Little Boy Blue,
Come blow your horn,
The sheep's in the meadow,
The cow's in the corn.
But where is the boy
Who looks after the sheep?
"He's under a haycock, fast asleep."
Will you wake him?
"No, not I,
For if I do,
He's sure to cry."

Diddle diddle dumpling,
My son John,
Went to bed
With his trousers on;
One shoe off,
And one shoe on,
Diddle diddle dumpling,
My son John.

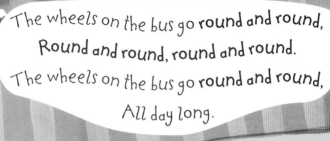

The wheels on the bus go **round and round,**
**Round** and **round, round and round.**
The wheels on the bus go **round and round,**
All day long.

The wipers on the bus go **swish swish swish,**
**Swish swish swish, swish swish swish.**
The wipers on the bus go **swish swish swish,**
All day long.

The horn on the bus goes **toot toot toot**,
**Toot toot toot, toot toot toot.**
The horn on the bus goes **toot toot toot**,
All day long.

Ring-a-ring o' roses,
A pocket full of posies,
A-tishoo! A-tishoo!
We all fall down.

Round and round the garden,

Like a teddy bear.

One step,

Two steps,

Tickle you under there!

Row, row, row your boat,

Gently down the stream;

Merrily, merrily, merrily, merrily,

Life is but a dream.

Hot cross buns!
Hot cross buns!
One a penny, two a penny,
Hot cross buns!

If you have no daughters,
Give them to your sons,
One a penny, two a penny,
Hot cross buns!

There was an old woman
Who lived in a shoe,
She had so many children
She didn't know what to do;
She gave them some broth
Without any bread;
Then scolded them soundly
And sent them to bed.

Pease porridge hot,
Pease porridge cold,
Pease porridge in the pot,
Nine days old.
Some like it hot,
Some like it cold,
Some like it in the pot,
Nine days old.

Jack be nimble, Jack be quick.

Jack jump over the candlestick.

See-saw, Margery Daw,
Johnny shall have a new master.
He shall have but a penny a day,
Because he can't work any faster.

Bobby Shafto's gone to sea,
Silver buckles on his knee;
He'll come back and marry me,
Bonny Bobby Shafto!

Bobby Shafto's bright and fair,
Combing down his yellow hair;
He's my love for evermore,
Bonny Bobby Shafto!

"Oranges and lemons,"
Say the bells of St Clement's.

"You owe me five farthings,"
Say the bells of St Martin's.

"When will you pay me?"
Say the bells of Old Bailey.

"When I grow rich,"
Say the bells of Shoreditch.

"Pray, when will that be?"
Say the bells of Stepney.

"I'm sure I don't know,"
Says the great bell at Bow.

Here comes a candle
To light you to bed.

Here comes a chopper
To chop off your head.

Tom, Tom, the piper's son,
Stole a pig and away did run;
The pig was eat
And Tom was beat,
And Tom went howling
Down the street.

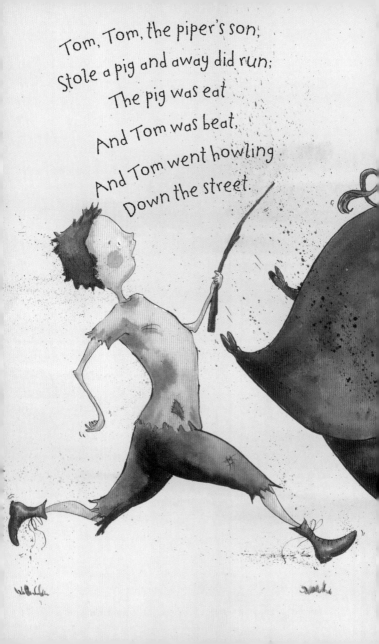

To market, to market, to buy a fat pig,
Home again, home again, jiggety jig;
To market, to market, to buy a fat hog,
Home again, home again, jiggety jog.

Little Tommy Tucker,

Sings for his supper:

What shall we give him?

White bread and butter.

How will he cut it

Without a knife?

How will he marry

Without a wife?

The man in the moon
Looked out of the moon,
And this is what he said:
"Now that I'm getting up, it's time
All children went to bed."

Good night, sleep tight,
Wake up bright in the morning light,
To do what's right with all your might.